Cyril Bonhamy

v

Madam Big

Jonathan Gathorne-Hardy

Cyril Bonhamy

v

Madam Big

Illustrations by Quentin Blake

Jonathan Cape
Thirty Bedford Square London

For Tom and Nell

First published 1981
Text © 1981 by Jonathan Gathorne-Hardy
Illustrations © 1981 by Quentin Blake

Jonathan Cape Ltd, 30 Bedford Square, London WC1

British Library Cataloguing in Publication Data

Gathorne-Hardy, Jonathan
Cyril Bonhamy v. Madam Big.
I. Title
823'.914[J]   PZ7

ISBN 0-224-01991-0

Photoset by Rowland Phototypesetting Ltd
and printed in Great Britain by
St Edmundsbury Press, Bury St Edmunds, Suffolk

Contents

Cyril Gets a Job

"You've got to get a job, Cyril," said his wife Deirdre suddenly at breakfast one day.

"Why?" said Cyril looking up reluctantly from the very interesting book he was reading.

"Because we haven't any money," said Deirdre in a high voice. "We haven't had any money for weeks. I owe money to all the shops."

It seemed to Cyril that Deirdre was always saying they hadn't any money. But it was true things were getting difficult. There was an oil stove in Cyril's study, where he spent all his time with his books; and an oil stove in the kitchen, where Deirdre spent all her time. The rest of the big old house in Wimbledon was freezing. Every day Deirdre came back saying yet another shop had refused to serve her. And Cyril had once loved his breakfasts. He would eat several eggs and plates of sausages, and then lots of toast. This morning the only thing to eat had been one

7

small boiled cabbage.

Today Deirdre made it seem all his fault, though he was doing his best. However, he longed to get back to his book, so he decided to soothe her.

"Don't worry, darling," he said, "it will soon be all right. I'm writing another book."

"A BOOK!" screamed Deirdre at the top of her voice, making Cyril jump. Then, because she was in fact very proud of Cyril being a writer, she said more gently, "But a book will take months, even years, Cyril. We need money *now*."

"Well, anyway," said Cyril, beginning to feel rather trapped, "what could I do? I'm not much good at anything except books."

"Nonsense," said Deirdre briskly. "In any case, there are lots of jobs you could do even if you are only good at books. Let's have a look at the ads in the *Wimbledon Star*."

Cyril watched nervously as Deirdre started to search through the large pages of their local paper. He didn't want a job. In particular, he didn't want the sort of job he imagined you'd find in the *Wimbledon Star*. But the silence continued. Clearly, it was not as easy as Deirdre thought. Cyril began to relax. He glanced down at his book. Soon he was reading peacefully again.

Some minutes later Deirdre announced in a sharp, pleased, loud voice, "Got it!"

"Got what?" said Cyril, startled.

"The very thing, the perfect job," said Deirdre. She looked at Cyril. "Yes – it would suit you down to the ground. I can just see you."

"I hope you realize I'm not strong," said Cyril, now thoroughly alarmed. "Remember my bad back. Remember my bad leg, my deafness."

"No – this is ideal," said Deirdre. "Perfect. You can be a Father Christmas."

"A *Father Christmas!*" cried Cyril, horrified. "Are you mad? Great sacks of toys, sledges, reindeer – I couldn't possibly. I'd stick in the chimneys. I won't."

"No, no, darling," said Deirdre, "not a real Father Christmas. Listen, I'll read what it says."

It seemed that Boringes, the large department store, was advertising for five Father Christmases. One night a week, each Father Christmas would have to take a turn helping the night watchman.

"It says 'free uniform'," said Deirdre excitedly, "and Cyril, the wages – £65 a week. And I'm sure it wouldn't be hard work. You could read your books. When it was your turn to be night watchman you could write."

"Well, I don't know," said Cyril, feeling very reluctant. "Those heavy sacks. I suppose, if it meant *no* chimneys. But I hate beards."

"Please, Cyril," said Deirdre. "Think of the £65. It's only for the next two weeks; till Christmas."

"Oh – all right," said Cyril.

When he set off that afternoon, a book under his arm for the journey, Deirdre kissed him tenderly goodbye. "And anyway, Cyril, you love children."

"I do not love children," said Cyril irritably.

"Well, don't say that or you'll never get the job," said Deirdre, feeling slightly less tender. "*Pretend*

9

you love them."

Boringes was in one of the grandest parts of London. It was ten storeys high, and seemed about a mile long. It seemed even longer because a huge block of flats was attached to it. Cyril went up to a tall man in a uniform standing importantly in front of the large double doors in the middle of the enormous building.

"I've come about the Father Christmas job advertised in the *Wimbledon Star*," he said.

"Round the back," said the man in uniform, not looking at him. "Join the queue."

Cyril walked slowly past the huge plate glass windows of Boringes. So there was a queue. It hadn't occurred to him there might be a lot of people wanting to be Father Christmas. Somehow, he'd thought he had only to turn up and the job was his. He began to feel a little less gloomy.

When he reached the back of Boringes and saw the queue he started to feel quite cheerful. About sixty men stretched along the pavement, and there must have been many more because the line disappeared down some steps under a sign saying "Staff". All, to Cyril, looked in their different ways perfect for the part of Father Christmas. But he did think the man behind him might have been rather an odd choice. He was one of the biggest men Cyril had ever seen. He was about six feet six inches tall, all bulgy and red, with a bristly chin and broken teeth. "Quite a lot of people after the job," Cyril said to him.

"There may be, matey," said the ugly giant, "but they're wasting their time. You see that big feller just going down the steps ahead?" He pointed up the queue, and Cyril saw another man with a dark beard, and almost as large as the first one, disappearing from sight. "Well – three of the lads have been chosen already. That's two to go. He'll get the next one, and I'll get the last. I'm not at liberty to say – but you don't stand a chance."

Cyril was delighted to hear it. He didn't mind if some sort of trickery was going on as long as it stopped him getting the job.

As they shuffled forward in the winter sunshine, he noticed a small cradle swinging in the air just above their heads. A man in it was cleaning the large windows of Boringes. Cyril watched him push a small lever from side to side to make the cradle move up and down. It looked rather fun.

It certainly seemed as though the business of choosing a Father Christmas could be done quickly because the queue moved rapidly forward. Soon they were at the top of the steps marked "Staff". And all the while, a constant stream of failed Father Christmases poured past them with gloomy faces.

At the bottom of the steps was a short corridor, then a large room. This had a door at the far end at which the queue stopped. Every minute or so a voice shouted "Next", and the next man would disappear to be interviewed. Disappear – and then almost at once reappear with a disappointed face, and set off up the steps again.

But Cyril had only been in the long room for a few moments when, at its far end, he saw the big tall man with the black beard vanish through the door. He was gone some time, and when he came back he was smiling broadly. Instead of going back to the street he pushed his way through the queue and went out through another door at the side of the room. As he did so, he turned towards the huge man behind Cyril and gave him a big wink.

It was clear now that something crooked was going on. Cyril didn't care. As far as he was concerned, the more crooked the better. The man in front of Cyril was called in, and almost instantly reappeared. "Splendid," thought Cyril and stepped confidently into a dark corridor, brushed past a bulky figure standing close to the door, and through another door immediately opposite.

It was the office of Mr Jessop, because on the desk was a strip of white card with "Mr Jessop" on it in black letters. Mr Jessop, with a pointed face like a rat, looked up. "Don't bother to shut the door," he said. "Sit down. Name?"

"Cyril Bonhamy," said Cyril. Mr Jessop wrote this down.

"Have you any experience of this sort of work, Mr Bonhamy?"

"None at all," said Cyril happily. "Never done anything like it in my life. I've never even worn a beard."

"Well, I don't think we need trouble you further, Mr Bonhamy," said Mr Jessop, "if you'll . . ."

But before he could finish, there came the sound of someone bursting into the room, and an angry voice spoke from behind Cyril. "What is the meaning of this, Mr Jessop? I've listened to you for the last five minutes and there's no rhyme or reason in it. That chap just now – one of the top ten Father Christmases last year, I heard him say. Number three a year ago. A natural for Boringes. And now you turn down this good man because he brings a fresh eye to the job. Eh?"

Mr Jessop had stood up. "I'm sorry, Mr Prichard," he said nervously.

"What's wrong with this good man?" boomed Mr Prichard behind Cyril's head.

"Well, he's a bit on the small side," said Mr Jessop.

"Small?" cried Mr Prichard. "We don't want a crowd of giants tramping about Boringes. These men are for children, for babes. We *need* some small ones."

"But it's the uniforms, Mr Prichard," said Mr Jessop, "the uniforms are on the large side."

"Large side – small side – you know the Boringes motto," said Mr Prichard. "'The Boringes Service knows no limit.' We'll *alter* the uniforms if needs be, Mr Jessop. Now, my good man," continued Mr Prichard stepping round so that Cyril could see he was plump and red, with a lot of carefully brushed grey hair, "now, my good man – what is your name?"

"Cyril Bonhamy," said Cyril, faintly irritated by all the "my good man" talk.

"Bonhamy!" cried Mr Prichard. "Bonhamy for Boringes! A natural! Tell me, Bonhamy – you like children?"

"I love them," said Cyril without enthusiasm, but remembering what Deirdre had said.

"Excellent," said Mr Prichard. "And what do you do with them? You have skills, no doubt?"

"Well . . ." said Cyril blankly.

"Yes, yes," encouraged Mr Prichard. "You chuck them under the chin, no doubt, dandle them on your knee? Eh?"

"That's right," said Cyril.

"Excellent," said Mr Prichard, "quite excellent. Can't have too much dandling and chucking. And what have you done in the past, Bonhamy?"

"I'm a writer," said Cyril. "I write books."

"A writer!" Mr Prichard almost shouted, raising his hands in delight. "That clinches it. 'Service with a story.' You can tell your stories to the little children. This is our man, Mr Jessop. Our search is over."

"But, Mr Prichard . . ." began Mr Jessop. He looked, for some reason, terrified.

"But, Mr Prichard . . ." began Cyril, wanting to explain that he wrote books for grown-ups, and there could be no question of his telling stories to children, and in fact he'd decided he didn't after all want to be a Father Christmas, and so goodbye.

"No buts," said Mr Prichard before Cyril could say any of this. "No ifs. Let us both congratulate Boringes' new Father Christmas, Mr Jessop – Boringes' *Senior* Father Christmas. Now, Mr Bonhamy, come with me." And Mr Prichard swept out, followed by a miserable Cyril, who was slowly realizing the full horror of what had happened – that he had, after all, despite his efforts and hopes, been given the ghastly job of Father Christmas.

Mr Prichard paused for a moment to address the

long line of men still queuing. "I'm sorry, gentlemen, but the last post has been filled. Would you please leave quietly. Thank you for coming." Next, he took Cyril along to the dressing room. Here, standing and smoking, were the four other Father Christmases. Each about seven feet tall, they looked to Cyril's gloomy eyes no more than a bunch of crooks.

When they saw Cyril, they stared at him with looks of amazement. At last one of them, the one with the black beard, said to Mr Prichard, "Excuse me, sir, but hasn't there been some mistake?"

"No mistake," said Mr Prichard. "Here is Mr Bonhamy – your fellow Father Christmas."

"But Mr Jessop said," went on the black-bearded man, "as how – on account of the uniforms . . ."

"Oh Mr Jessop and the uniforms," said Mr Prichard. "Uniforms can be altered. Uniforms can be shortened. The uniforms don't look too big to me."

In fact, hanging from high hooks in a line along the wall, the uniforms looked enormous. From each hook dangled a long pair of red trousers, a large red jacket with a hood, both edged with some white artificial fur, and a long thick false beard. A pair of black gum boots stood against the wall under each kit.

Yet large as they were, two of the men chosen by Mr Jessop could scarcely cram themselves into their uniforms. Their great red arms bulged out of the sleeves, which now seemed too short; the red hoods couldn't cover their heads; the beards became wisps on their own bristling chins.

Cyril, on the other hand, simply vanished inside his uniform. The sleeves and trousers were at least two feet too long, while the jacket brushed the floor all round him like a skirt, and the beard reached well below his waist. He felt absolutely ridiculous. "I can't possibly wear this stupid thing," he said, his voice muffled from inside the hood.

"Of course you can't," cried Mr Prichard. "Just what I'd expect you to say. You're an actor, Mr Bonhamy, an artist. You want to look the part. And some of those other jackets need to be longer. Get out of them, gentlemen, while I have a word with Miss Pringle in Sewing."

It took Cyril some time to struggle free from his Father Christmas uniform. When he did, a rather frightening sight met his eyes.

The four men were standing round him in a circle. They looked extremely big and extremely fierce. As he finally pulled himself out of the long red trousers, one of the men said to the bearded one, "Give it to 'im, Pete."

"Look here, little man," said Pete, putting his face down close so that Cyril could see that the skin behind the black beard was covered in bumps and scars, "Look here, little fellow – there's been a mistake. You don't want to be no Father Christmas. So you won't be needing those any more." And at this Pete rudely pulled Cyril's uniform out of his arms. "If you know what's good for you, matey," said Pete, his nose practically touching Cyril's, "you'll scarper, buzz off, right now."

Cyril felt frightened; at the same time he found

Pete irritating. And he'd been through rather a lot that morning, what with all that "my good man" talk and so on. "I don't see how there's been a mistake," he said. "I don't particularly want this silly job, but I'm certainly not giving it up to please you. So thank you very much and I'll have my uniform back." And reaching up Cyril bravely snatched back his clothes again.

At this, all the men looked at each other and then bunched up closer. Pete bent down and put one huge red hand on Cyril's shoulder. "So that's how you want it, little man," he said. "You want to play it rough, eh?"

To Cyril's intense relief he heard at this ugly moment the now familiar booming of Mr Prichard. "Aha," cried Mr Prichard, "getting to know each other. Splendid. Now come along and I'll leave you with Miss Pringle."

Cyril, however, felt that the quicker he got away from Pete the better. "Thank you, Mr Prichard," he said, "but Mrs Bonhamy is very good at sewing. She can do it over the weekend." And without waiting he gathered his uniform to his chest and hurried to the door.

"Very well," he heard Mr Prichard calling, "sharp at eight on Monday. My office on the Fifth Floor."

Deirdre was so pleased he had got the job that Cyril began to feel slightly less gloomy. She talked such a lot about the books he could read and the writing he could do that he began to feel there'd be hardly any Father Christmasing at all.

"The other Father Christmases don't seem to like

me much," he said.

"You must get to know them," said Deirdre. "We'll ask them round for supper at the weekend."

"Perhaps," said Cyril, not thinking this would do a lot of good.

That night they had the first proper meal for weeks – roast chicken, little sausages, bread sauce and roast potatoes.

Sinister Doings at Boringes

Deirdre worked all weekend on Cyril's uniform and when he left it was still too large but didn't look ridiculous. The final thing she did was cut his beard in half.

"Don't you think you'll look a bit odd on the Underground?" she said, as he set off into the winter darkness at seven o'clock on Monday morning.

"I don't see why," said Cyril, hitching his sack of books higher on to his shoulder. "There must be masses of Father Christmases around at this time of the year." He did not want to worry Deirdre but he'd determined he would not allow himself to be left alone for an instant with Pete and his fellow crooks. This meant avoiding the dressing room.

Although he did in fact attract a good deal of attention among the early rush hour passengers, and some laughter, he was far too busy reading to notice.

Five of the ten floors at Boringes were to have a living Father Christmas, and the most important floor was the Fourth. This was Cyril's floor. The

Toy Department was here, and at the centre of the Toy Department was Wendy City. To Cyril this appeared to be just a bunch of tiny, flimsy wooden houses with plastic curtains, arranged in a square. But opposite was the Father Christmas Grotto.

Mr Prichard showed him round personally. "Mr Jessop is your Floor Manager," he said, as he led Cyril through a dark blue plastic tunnel covered in glitter and lit by coloured lights. "But I keep a special eye on Wendy City and the Grotto. Now here," said Mr Prichard as they came to the end of the tunnel, "here, Mr Bonhamy, is your sledge!"

Cyril looked without interest at a large, false-looking white plastic sledge. Inside it was a sack.

"We provide the toys," said Mr Prichard. "I noticed you'd brought your own. Very thoughtful."

"These are books," said Cyril.

"Ah," said Mr Prichard, "for you to read stories from, I suppose."

Cyril didn't answer.

There were two entrances to Father Christmas Grotto. One said "A Present from Father Christmas – 25p"; and the other said "Present and *Story* from Father Christmas – 75p". Most of the time Cyril was to sit in the sledge and hand out presents from the sack; if someone came through the story tunnel he was to tell a story as well. Cyril looked back at the story notice as they left this entrance. "That will have to go," he thought grimly.

"Every now and again, take a walk," said Mr Prichard. "Chuck a few chins, even do some dandling." Here Mr Prichard took a plastic Father Christmas and bounced it up and down on his knee once or twice, smiling at Cyril. Cyril tried to smile back.

Wherever they went there seemed to be Father Christmases – plastic ones, plaster ones, paper ones, there were even some life-sized cardboard Father Christmases on wheels which the assistants could push to important places. "A lot of Father Christmases," said Cyril. "Almost too many, I'd say."

"Well, it's our theme," said Mr Prichard. "But, Mr Bonhamy, the Boringes service knows no limit."

In one respect, the Boringes service seemed downright dangerous to Cyril, though, along with Wendy City and the Grotto, it was what Mr Prichard called a highlight.

In the middle of all ten floors at Boringes was a wide circular well, a space which reached from the ground floor to the roof. From the Fifth Floor there had been suspended across this well what looked like one enormous loop of a switchback. This swooped down to the level of the Third Floor, and then up to the Fourth. Children under ten were given a mat for 30p, shoved out on to the switchback, went shooting down, then up, and landed – quite safely according to Mr Prichard – on a platform at the very gates of Wendy City (entrance fee 40p).

"Finally, Mr Bonhamy," said Mr Prichard, "here is a plan of the Fourth Floor. Every two hours I want you to go to these spots in the order they are marked on the plan. There will then be an announcement on the store broadcasting system and you'll give a *free* present to the first ten children to reach you."

"Oh Lord," said Cyril gloomily. The whole job

sounded more boring every minute.

"You think it over-generous?" said Mr Prichard. "Mr Bonhamy, remember – *the Boringes service knows no limit.*"

When he got back to the Grotto, Cyril climbed on to a chair and ripped down the notice saying "Present and *Story* from Father Christmas – 75p" and stuffed it into a waste-paper basket. Then he went and settled himself on his sledge and began to read.

So began Cyril's short life as a Father Christmas. He soon found it would have been perfectly all right if it hadn't been for the children. No sooner was he well into his book than some irritating brat would come in wanting a present. After a while, Cyril just left the sack open and said without looking up, "Help yourself."

It was Mr Jessop who stopped this. He was passing the Grotto when he was amazed to see a child of six staggering out with its arms piled high with plastic trumpets, plastic axes, plastic space guns, plastic dolls' clothes.

"You can't do that," he stormed at Cyril, who was looking irritably up at him from his book. "It's one present for 25p."

"25p for this piffle?" said Cyril, giving the emptying sack a shake. "Monstrous. Anyway, I thought there was no limit to the Boringes service."

"There's a limit to no limit," said Mr Jessop. "And who took down the notice outside the story entrance?"

"I haven't the faintest idea," said Cyril. "And now would you please go? I'm busy."

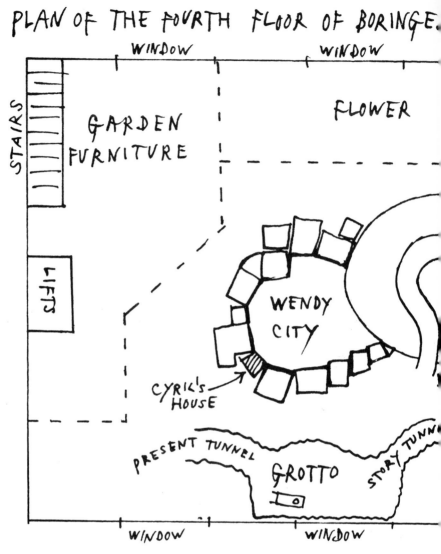

WINDOW WINDOW

STAIRS

GARDEN FURNITURE

FLOWER

LIFTS

WENDY CITY

CYRIL'S HOUSE

PRESENT TUNNEL

GROTTO

STORY TUNNEL

WINDOW WINDOW

"If you are going to be rude, Bonhamy," said Mr Jessop, "I shall sack you. Nothing would give me greater pleasure."

Cyril ignored him. A little later he heard faint tapping coming from the end of the story tunnel, and soon after this a little boy appeared and said, "Story please, Father Christmas." Cyril gave him an armful of flimsy plastic presents instead of a story, and then

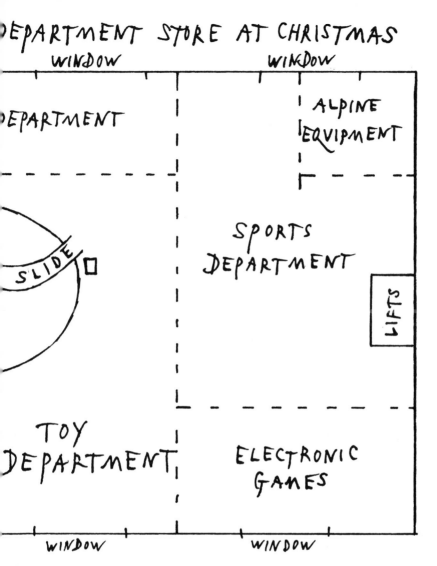

WINDOW   WINDOW

DEPARTMENT   ALPINE
                              EQUIPMENT

SLIDE   SPORTS
                         DEPARTMENT

                                        LIFTS

TOY
DEPARTMENT   ELECTRONIC
                         GAMES

WINDOW   WINDOW

led him out of the other tunnel. He carried his now nearly empty sack because it was time for the first ten children to try and reach him at the entrance to the Sports Department.

Outside, as he had expected, he found that a large new cardboard notice had been nailed up announcing "Present and *Story* from Father Christmas – 75p". Underneath it stood Mr Jessop. "I don't think they'll miss *that*, Bonhamy," he said as Cyril passed. Cyril didn't even bother to reply.

The handout at the Sports Department was a nightmare. After the announcement over the store broadcasting system, about seventy small children closed in on Cyril. He gave plastic presents to the first ten and then had to fight his way free. Several children got knocked over and began to cry. One mother went to find someone to complain to.

When he arrived back at the Grotto, Mr Jessop had gone and there were small queues at each tunnel. Cyril dismissed these and standing on the chair managed with some difficulty to tear down the new "Present and *Story*" notice. This was too large for the waste-paper basket, and tucking it under his arm he hurried across into Wendy City to see if he could find somewhere to hide it.

Cyril found he rather enjoyed Wendy City. Pushing into first one, then another of the flimsy plastic or wood-and-canvas houses, he thought, a man could be lost for weeks in here. The little houses were clustered in a group with one side along the balcony. They were arranged in such a way that Cyril felt there must be a space in the middle into which he could creep and perhaps make a comfortable hideaway – but there seemed no way in.

However, on the very far edge there was one tiny brown Wendy House – meant to look like a loaf of bread – which was half hidden by a much larger fort. Cyril concealed the cardboard notice inside it. When he came out he was looking very thoughtful.

After this, he stood and watched the children on

the switchback. It looked terrifying. Sliding out on their stomachs from the Fifth Floor, they swooped down out of sight and then shot up again to land with a thump on a small platform beside the entrance to Wendy City. Every now and again an assistant came and carried away the mats on which they slid.

When Cyril got back to the Grotto he found another queue of children and a furious Mr Jessop. "Where have you been, Bonhamy?"

"Doing my duty," said Cyril. "Patrolling the Fourth Floor."

"You've been gone half an hour," said Mr Jessop.

"It takes half an hour," said Cyril.

"Furthermore," said Mr Jessop, "I had a complaint that you took a swipe at a child with your sack. You knocked him over."

"I daresay I did," said Cyril. "I was lucky to escape with my life."

"And where is the new notice I had put up about the story?'

"I haven't the faintest idea," said Cyril.

Mr Jessop took a deep breath. "This is your last chance, Bonhamy; If I have one other complaint I shall go to Mr Prichard and see that you are sacked."

"I need another lot of those ridiculous presents," said Cyril, handing Mr Jessop the empty sack. "And kindly don't call me Bonhamy. It is extremely rude." He didn't feel in the least alarmed by Mr Jessop, though he realized he would have to keep an eye open for Mr Prichard.

That evening, as he was about to leave Boringes, he saw that Pete and the three other Father Christ-

27

mases, no longer in uniform, were lounging about under the street lamp outside the staff entrance. Now, they may not be waiting for me, thought Cyril; on the other hand, perhaps they are. He hurried back into the store and was just in time to leave by the front entrance before it was locked.

Supper that night was once again delicious. They had the rest of the chicken minced up and fried with crisps and a treacle tart with cream. Cyril, who hated getting up early, went to bed at half-past nine.

The next morning he left the house even earlier than the day before – at six o'clock. There were various things he had to do and he wanted to do them before anyone arrived at Boringes.

The staff entrance was unlocked at half-past six for the cleaners. Cyril hurried through the empty store and up to the Fourth Floor. His arms were filled with rugs, cushions and various other things to make his life more comfortable. These he put in the little Wendy House which looked like a loaf of bread. On the door of this he pinned a notice:"NO ENTRY – UNDER REPAIR", and for greater safety fixed padlocks inside and out. He then went and pinned a notice, which he had also prepared the night before, outside each of the entrances to the Father Christmas Grotto. These said "Queue Here". Then he returned to the Wendy House, locked himself in, settled among the rugs and cushions and tried to go to sleep.

This wasn't at all easy, and after dozing fitfully, Cyril was finally forced fully awake at five to ten by all the clattering and thumping and general noise. But it was just as well because at ten o'clock, according to Mr Prichard's map, Father Christmas was supposed to be standing in the Garden Furniture Department. Cyril had a simple plan to deal with this. He wheeled one of the large cardboard Father Christmases into the middle of the Department and put a sack containing ten plastic presents at its foot. He hung the third notice he had made round the Father Christmas's neck. It said "First ten take one present each".

When he got back to the Grotto, Cyril found yet another notice – wood this time, and screwed in – had been put above the "Present and *Story*" tunnel. This had attracted a small queue of mothers and children. Cyril said story-telling had been cancelled and sent them to join the "Present" queue.

It only took him about five minutes to get rid of them all. Sitting in the sledge, he made the children come in quickly, one at a time, and put 25p into the box. Then he gave them each a present from the sack and sent them packing.

"Hurry up," called Cyril. "Faster. Next! Come on, quickly – next, next! Next! Next!" Plastic doll's clothes, plastic noses, plastic space helmets, plastic pencils which wouldn't write, plastic penknives which wouldn't cut – the children ran in, then ran out. "What's this supposed to be?" said one angry little boy, holding a handful of plastic sticks. "Get out!" shouted Cyril. "Next! Next!"

One mother came in and complained she'd been waiting over an hour. "I can't help that, madam," said Cyril. Another mother complained at the speed. "You didn't have a word to say to my poor Laura," she said. "You just shouted 'Next' at her."

"What do you expect for 25p?" said Cyril irritably. "There's a limit to the Boringes service, you know."

Both mothers went to find someone else to complain to. Cyril returned to his Wendy House and settled himself comfortably into the cushions with a book. Everything was going very well indeed.

At eleven o'clock he picked up his sack and prepared to return to the Grotto. But outside, happening to glance away towards the lifts, he saw a sight which first stopped him dead – and next sent him scurrying back into the Wendy House.

In the distance, he had seen Mr Prichard and Mr Jessop. Mr Prichard was listening; Mr Jessop was waving his arms and talking. Several times he pointed at the Grotto.

Cyril hurried to the story tunnel. In his hand he now had a book, *Fairy Tales for the Under-Fives*. At the head of the queue stood a large fat boy of about fourteen, nearly as tall as Cyril himself. "Come on, little boy," he said, "come and have a story."

"Huh?" grunted the boy.

Cyril took his arm. "This way," he said. Oh dear, he thought to himself, I've got a half-wit.

In the sledge, he managed after some difficulty to settle the huge half-wit on to his knee. Then, opening *Fairy Tales for the Under-Fives* he began to read. "Once upon a time there was a little girl called Red Riding-Hood . . ."

It was this touching scene that Mr Prichard beheld as he peeped into the Grotto.

31

" . . . and little Red Riding-Hood lived happily ever after," finished Cyril. He heaved the boy off his knee and, searching in the sack, produced a plastic whistle. "There you are, little fellow," he said. "Now – please tell the next in the queue to come in."

Mr Prichard now appeared, followed by an angry-looking Mr Jessop. "That was a pleasure to watch," said Mr Prichard. "But, Mr Bonhamy, I fear there has been a complaint. I understand you've been using a dummy Father Christmas for the announced appearances."

"Well – the Grotto is so popular," said Cyril, "the queues so long, I thought it more important to deal with them."

"The queues are long because you are never here," burst in Mr Jessop. "You've been away for an hour."

"I have to patrol the whole of the Fourth Floor," said Cyril.

"Quite so," said Mr Prichard. "I think we can assume Mr Bonhamy is doing his best. Carry on, Mr Bonhamy. Mr Jessop – I'd like a word with you."

Outside, he spoke firmly. "I want no more complaints about Mr Bonhamy," he said. "You were against him from the start. The man sees no limit to his services. A Boringes man. That will be all."

So Cyril might have been safe till Christmas had there not occurred, on the very same day, three very sinister events indeed.

Returning to the Grotto after an hour's reading in the Wendy House, he found a note nailed to the sledge. The writing was in rough capital letters: "GET OUT OF THIS STORE BY 1 O'CLOCK OR YOUR A GONER."

Cyril ate a nervous lunch in the Wendy House. What should he do? Perhaps he should leave – yet he knew Deirdre would be very upset. After all, what could happen to him?

At four o'clock Cyril wheeled the cardboard Father Christmas in between the Sports Department and the Flower Department. There was rebuilding work going on here and Cyril placed the Father Christmas up against the scaffolding which reached to the ceiling.

When he returned to collect it at twenty past four, a terrible sight met his eyes. A cement mixer had fallen from the top of the scaffolding straight down on to the cardboard Father Christmas.

It had been smashed to pieces. Cyril stared at it in horror.

"If I'd been there I'd have been killed," he said.

The workmen agreed. "You had a lucky escape, mate," said one.

Nor could they explain how the mixer had fallen. It had been safe enough when they went for their tea. When they returned – this. The foreman spread his hands in horror.

Still worse was to follow. Cyril left Boringes at half-past five, by a small side door he had discovered in the basement. The Underground was very crowded that night. Several trains stopped and went on, too full to take any more passengers. Cyril was standing fairly near the front of the packed platform, reading. As the next train came in some commotion started behind him and his book was jostled out of his hands. Bending quickly to pick it up, he felt a huge fist brush over his shoulder. Then there came cries and shrieks and the squealing of train brakes.

Cyril stood up. The man in front of him had fallen in front of the train. But there was now more shouting and commotion from farther up the platform. Cyril could see that some huge man, a giant, was pushing his way through the crowd to the exit. Before he disappeared he turned his head a little and Cyril glimpsed a black beard. Surely it was Pete, one of the awful Boringes Father Christmases.

Luckily the man who had fallen in front of the train was not badly hurt. He had missed the electric rail and the train had stopped in time. But Cyril was quite certain that it was he who was meant to be in front of the train. Pete had tried to push him.

"They're trying to murder me," he said.

"Oh surely not, darling," said Deirdre soothingly as she helped him out of his Father Christmas uniform. It was quite damp from the snow.

Cyril explained what had happened. "But no one could mistake a flat cardboard Father Christmas for you," said Deirdre, looking at the plump round figure of her agitated husband.

"Well – that may have been a warning," said Cyril. "And what about the Underground?"

"But you say it was very crowded," said Deirdre. "And are you certain it was this man Pete?"

"Well – not *certain*," admitted Cyril. But he was certain they were trying to kill him, though he couldn't think why. And, as he fell uneasily asleep that night, he also felt certain that the worst was yet to come.

Down the Chimney

Cyril had set the alarm for half-past four. He rose groggily from his bed, feeling there wasn't a great deal of point in getting into it at all for so short a time.

He'd decided that his safest course was to arrive at Boringes long before, and leave long after the other Father Christmases, who were, for some mad reason of their own, trying to murder him.

He even wondered if he should leave Boringes at all. Perhaps he should simply set up home in the Wendy House – with thirty tins of pilchards, say, and fifty or so packets of Rice Krispies. But in fact the Wendy House was already beginning to look rather squalid – what with crumbs and books and papers – and Cyril didn't feel he could stand it.

He reached Boringes at six o'clock and let himself in by the little side entrance he'd discovered.

But this time he found it completely impossible to get to sleep in the Wendy House. At half-past six the cleaning ladies were banging about outside, sweeping up. One rattled the door, trying to get in. Then at seven o'clock some workmen arrived to strengthen the switchback. Cyril could hear their drills and hammers even with his head under the cushions. At nine, the store opened and queues started to form at both entrances to the Grotto.

Cyril emerged blearily at ten o'clock. By now the sight of a crowd of children and their mothers roused him swiftly to fury. He shoved his way into the Grotto and started handing out presents as fast as he could.

"Next!" shouted Cyril. "Next! Next! Next!" The children scampered in – emerging in a few seconds, terrified and clutching plastic space weapons so feeble they usually broke as Cyril shovelled them out. The few brave enough to complain were chased from the Grotto with a length of lead piping left behind by the workmen.

One mother came in with her little boy crying inside a plastic space helmet. "I can't get it off," she wailed. "He's trapped."

"It's not my fault his head's too big," said Cyril. "Next!"

As the day wore on more and more mothers complained. Cyril either told them to shut up or ignored them. Several times they marched in a body to Mr Jessop, demanding their money back and threatening to call the police. Humbly, Mr Jessop apologized. Three times he went to Mr Prichard, only to be told that "Mr Bonhamy is the best Father Christmas Boringes has ever had". Mr Bonhamy, meanwhile, was asleep in his Wendy House.

When evening came and the store closed, Cyril faced fresh difficulties. He dared not leave at once for fear that one of the killer Father Christmases would see and follow him. At the same time, to remain behind was full of danger as well. Each night, one Father Christmas did duty as night watchman and patrolled the store. Cyril sat terrified in the Wendy House, not daring to leave.

But at half-past eight, having listened and looked carefully for ten minutes, he crept out and, keeping to the shadows, tiptoed round the edges of the Fourth Floor. He waited, listening another five minutes at the top of the stairs which led to his side entrance, then hurried down them and out into the night.

He was far too frightened to take the Underground again, and the bus took half an hour to come. Standing in his red uniform trying to read by the light of the street lamp Cyril looked rather a forlorn sight in the falling snow. Forlorn – but also rather odd.

He didn't get back to Wimbledon until half-past ten. Deirdre was getting more and more worried about him. "Look," she said, "you're falling asleep over supper again. Surely you needn't get up quite so early."

"You don't understand," said Cyril. "They're trying to kill me."

"I'm sure they're not, darling," said Deirdre. Cyril didn't answer but concentrated on keeping awake long enough to finish the roast lamb. He went

37

to bed immediately afterwards, at half-past eleven.

Cyril began to crack up next day. When his alarm went at half-past three, he felt he'd only just got into bed, which was indeed almost the case. Outside, it was pitch dark and snowing again. The Father Christmas uniform was warm and he wrapped the long white beard round his neck like a scarf. But what he chiefly wanted was sleep.

Yet once again the noise of cleaners and workmen kept waking him up at Boringes. He dozed uneasily until the familiar sound of the queue forming outside the Grotto penetrated the Wendy House. Cyril, gripped by a feeling of dull rage, shouldered the bag of plastic toys and stumped out to deal with them.

It took him ten minutes, but one little boy called Tom proved particularly difficult. He refused to accept the card of plastic dolls' dresses thrust at him by Cyril. "You take those – or you get nothing," said Cyril.

"I won't," said Tom.

"You will," said Cyril.

"Won't," said Tom.

In the end Cyril had to pick him up by his collar and carry him out bodily. He managed to resist a desire to hurl the horrid little boy over the balcony down to the ground floor.

That morning, however, when Mr Jessop was confronted by the usual band of furious mothers he did not, as normally, apologize and try and soothe them. He took them to see Mr Prichard. "Ladies," he said, wondering why on earth he hadn't done this before, "I think you must complain to the Store

Manager himself. Follow me."

Unaware of this danger, Cyril slumped into the sledge. He felt too tired to return to the Wendy House. He tucked the sack of toys behind his head as a pillow and in a moment was fast asleep.

It was this sleeping Father Christmas that Tom and four of his friends found five minutes later when they came creeping down the present tunnel. They had been told to wait quietly outside the Grotto while their mothers went to complain, and had grown bored. They gathered round the unconscious figure and stared. Then Tom suddenly took hold of Cyril's false beard, pulled it out two feet, which was as far as it would stretch, and let it go. With a loud *Snap!* it whipped back viciously against Cyril's bare skin.

The effect was electrifying. With a loud "Aaaah!" Cyril sprang to his feet. His chin felt on fire. He stood, swaying muzzily, brushing tears of pain from his eyes. Tom seized his chance and, yanking the beard hard down again, let it go with another whip-like *Snap!* against Cyril's smarting chin. "Aaaah!" cried Cyril. "*Aaah!*" Dancing about in front of him, tongues out and waggling their fingers in their ears, the five little boys went "Yahoo! Yahoo! Yahoo!"

And suddenly – hating being a Father Christmas, sick of loathsome little children, tormented by lack of sleep – a wave of fury swept Cyril. With a great cry of rage he jumped out of the sledge and whirling the sack of toys like a club he charged across the Grotto. Terrified, the little boys sped from him up the present tunnel. Cyril stopped, scrabbled in his

sack and flung toys after them – "Get out!" he yelled. "Get out!"

It was at this moment that Mr Prichard approached the Grotto from the outside. In amazement he saw the frightened little boys shoot out of the present tunnel. Toys were flying through the air behind them. From inside came the muffled cries of Boringes' Senior Father Christmas. His face grim, Mr Prichard pressed forward.

Half an hour later Cyril and he faced each other across the desk in Mr Prichard's office. Mr Prichard was very angry – but he was also puzzled.

"You were our best Father Christmas, Mr Bonhamy," he said. "What's happened?"

"I've been sleeping badly," said Cyril. "In fact, you could say I haven't been sleeping at all."

"But such a terrible change!" cried Mr Prichard. "I understand there's been a minimum of dandling and virtually no chucking at all. I wanted you to chuck till your fingers *ached*, Mr Bonhamy; dandle till your knees were *raw*. You understand?"

"Not a wink," went on Cyril, too tired to listen and giving a huge yawn. "Not a blink of sleep for weeks."

"For goodness' sake," said Mr Prichard crossly. "Father Christmases aren't *supposed* to sleep at this time of year. Act the part – you said you were an actor."

"I didn't," said Cyril. "You said that."

"Well, be an actor," said Mr Prichard. "Imagine you're Father Christmas. Get out on those roofs, get down those chimneys. *Become* Father Christmas."

41

"Roofs?" said Cyril with surprise. "Which roofs? Where?"

"Anywhere – there," said Mr Prichard gesturing irritably and vaguely over his shoulder. "Use your imagination."

"I can't climb roofs at my age," cried Cyril aghast. "You must be mad. I'd stick in the chimneys. I hate heights. How am I to get up there? You can't be serious."

"Oh yes, of course I'm serious," said Mr Prichard sarcastically. "We have a perfectly good mountain climbing department. Get some rope, get some climbing boots. No," said Mr Prichard standing up, "I'm afraid unless there is a very great improvement I shall be forced to sack you. I understand you are on night watchman duty tonight. A chance to shine, Mr Bonhamy! Take it."

Cyril stumped despairingly back to the Fourth Floor. He'd forgotten about being night watchman. What on earth was he to do? This was the ideal time for the other Father Christmases to murder him. His heart sank.

Somehow he got through the rest of the day. *Fairy Tales for the Under-Fives* went blurry before his eyes, the Grotto swarmed with beastly children, he longed for the Wendy House – but all the time Mr Jessop was watching him, spying.

If it hadn't been for Mr Jessop Cyril would simply have gone home, delighted to get the sack. But the thought of how pleased Mr Jessop would be irritated him so much he thought he'd try and stick it out.

By the time evening came and the store closed he

was in a complete panic about being murdered. Sitting terrified in the Wendy House, he'd almost decided to spend the whole night there and risk being caught not night watching, when he heard someone calling him.

"Mr Bonhamy," came a voice from outside. "You there, Mr Bonhamy?"

Cyril didn't move. So they thought he'd just walk straight out and let them drop a wheelbarrow on to his head, did they? He wasn't going to be caught like that, thank you very much.

However, the voice didn't sound at all like Pete or any of the other giant Father Christmases. It was very high and shaky. "Mr Bonhamy," it called again.

Cyril tiptoed to the door and put his eye to the rather large gap above the hinges. A small man in a cap and scarf was standing outside the Grotto. Was it a trap? "Mr Bonhamy?" called the man again. "Mr Bonhamy – please."

Very cautiously, Cyril opened the door a few inches and put his head out. "Yes?" he said.

The little man, who had a pink face and curly grey hair under his cap, came hurrying over. "Glad to meet you, Mr Bonhamy. Fred's the name. Senior Night Watchman."

"Do you mean there are *two* of us?" said Cyril.

"That's it," said Fred. "I take the basement and Floors One to Five; you take the last five floors and the roof."

"What about the other Father Christmases?" said Cyril, still thinking of knives in the back and falling concrete mixers.

"They left on the dot of five-thirty tonight," said Fred. "A bit unusual."

"You're quite sure?" said Cyril. "How do you know they're not lurking about downstairs somewhere?"

"There's no one there," said Fred. "I've done me rounds once already."

"Well, what about this roof?" said Cyril. "Did you say I had to get on the roof? I can't possibly do that. I hate heights."

"It's dead easy," said Fred. He gave Cyril maps of all the floors. He only had to visit the roof once. The entrance was up some stairs beside the lifts on the Tenth Floor. Cyril had to walk out about thirty yards, turn right and there was a large chimney. A box was fixed to it, and inside this was a piece of paper Cyril had to sign to show he'd been there. That was all.

When Fred had gone, Cyril threw away all the maps except that of the roof. He was far too tired for night watching, but he would just sign that bit of paper. Then he would spend the night sleeping in the Wendy House.

But there was one thing to do first. He realized that Mr Prichard had been joking about going down chimneys. No doubt he'd been joking about the climbing equipment too, but in fact it might be a good idea to have a few ropes and things on the roof. Cyril set off wearily for the end of the Fourth Floor.

To his surprise he found the equipment rather interesting – shining ice axes, gleaming gas cylinders, strange clips and pins. He picked up a huge

44

pair of boots covered in metal teeth and dropped them into the toy sack, also a heavy alpine torch. Next, a handsome nylon rope, a bundle of crampons and an ice pick caught his fancy. Then he saw a fine high-altitude oxygen mask complete with cylinders. Breathing could well be a problem. Finally, for luck, he tossed in several bunches of assorted hooks, clamps and crimps.

He returned to the Wendy House for a bit of supper before setting out. But the sight of the cushions was too much for him. Settling himself full length, he closed his eyes and in a moment was fast asleep.

Cyril woke with a jump five hours later. He felt much better, though extremely hungry. But he thought he ought to get on with his climbing before much later. He'd have the sausage rolls Deirdre had prepared when he got back.

Just before he left, however, something rather odd happened. He had shoved the mountain climbing equipment back in his sack and was swinging the ice pick over his head to get the feel of it, when the point went into the wall of the Wendy House behind him. To his surprise, he saw a light shining through the hole the point had made. Pressing his eye to this hole, Cyril found he was looking into a small room in the middle of Wendy City, its walls made from the backs of all the Wendy Houses. Cyril could not see a great deal, but what he could see surprised him. There was a map on one wall covered in flags; he could see some radio equipment and also three telephones.

"Odd place to have an office," thought Cyril.

However, he was already hours late, so he stuffed some newspaper into the hole, shouldered his sack and set out.

Standing in the doorway on to the roof, the expedition didn't seem "dead easy" at all. It was cold and had started snowing again. Although there was some light from the street lamps far below, little of it reached into the darkness on the top of Boringes. Black shapes of chimneys and sloping roofs loomed around him, snow blown between them by the wind.

Also the air was thin so high up. It was quite definitely difficult to breathe. Cyril struggled into the oxygen mask and adjusted the heavy cylinders on his back, and as he did so the map slipped from his hand and vanished in the wind. The oxygen equipment made it easier to breathe but more difficult to see, especially as the snow settled on the mask's goggles. Brushing it away, he set off nervously into the night.

Cyril seemed to wander over the roofs of Boringes for hours. Within ten minutes he became hopelessly lost. In the swirling snow, the shapes and chimneys all looked the same. Sometimes he could see almost nothing at all. He clambered over walls and fell down in gutters. Once, thinking he saw the large chimney Fred had mentioned on top of a sloping roof, he somehow dragged himself half way up before his strength gave out and he slipped noisily and painfully back into the gutter again.

Cyril lay panting. If there hadn't been a parapet round the roof of Boringes he'd have slid straight into the street below. The sack of toys and equipment weighed a ton. He struggled up, reached inside and threw a few handfuls of crimps and clamps out into the night. Why couldn't Mr Prichard night watch his own silly roofs?

Half an hour later Cyril had had enough. He'd decided the only thing to do was to bash a hole through the tiles with the ice pick and just force his way back as best he could. But at this moment he stumbled into something that seemed to offer an easier way to escape.

It was a low chimney surrounded by scaffolding. But shining his torch and brushing the snow from his goggles, it seemed to Cyril it was large enough to climb down.

In fact he'd left the roof of Boringes long ago, and had for some time been wandering on top of the enormous block of flats attached to the department store. The chimney had been widened because a large new gas boiler and air-conditioning system was being fitted.

Cyril took out the colossal pair of climbing boots with the metal teeth, and found he could fit them over his gum boots. Chimney or not, he didn't care. All he wanted was to get off the roof. If it led to a bedroom, then he'd give away some presents. That at least would please Mr Prichard. He tied one end of the nylon rope round his waist and the other end to the scaffolding.

It was very difficult to walk. Cyril could scarcely lift the huge boots, which clanked loudly at each step. With great difficulty, he managed to get his legs

inside the chimney and then, turning on his stomach and holding the sack in one hand and the rope in the other, he began to lower himself down.

But the boots were far too heavy. There was a pause while Cyril balanced at the top – then all at once he vanished. He slithered ten feet down the chimney and stopped with a jolt. He tried to force himself further down, but it was impossible. Next he tried to pull himself up by the rope, but it simply untied itself and came tumbling on to his head.

He seemed to be stuck. Staring up through the oxygen mask he could see nothing. "Mr Prichard," he called, his voice muffled, "I think I'm stuck." He swung his legs and felt the big boots biff against the chimney side.

He *was* stuck. Now Cyril began to panic. He kicked violently with his boots and beat with his hands, against the chimney. "Help! Help! Help!" he shouted. "Boringes! Deirdre! Help!"

And then one of his boots drove a hole in the side of the old chimney. Immediately, Cyril broke into a frenzy of kicking and shouting. He felt another brick give way and then another – and suddenly with a rumble of tumbling bricks the whole side of the chimney collapsed and with a whoosh Cyril found he was falling swiftly and noisily into the darkness below.

Enter Madam Big

In Flat 32, one of the luxury ones at the top of the block adjoining Boringes, Mr and Mrs Salt were about to turn out the light and go to sleep. "It's beautiful, darling," said Mrs Salt.

She was pointing, for the fourth or fifth time that night, to the lovely new "log effect" electric fire they had just had put into their fireplace. Mr Salt agreed – it was beautiful.

But then Mrs Salt sat up and put her little head with its fluffy golden hair on one side. "What's that noise, darling?" she said.

Mr Salt listened. There did seem to be some vague but persistent sound in the chimney. "Just the wind, darling," he said. "Perhaps some little robin sheltering from the snow."

"Little *robin*?" said Mrs Salt, now rather alarmed. There had come a distinct rattling and then a sharp loud sound of something heavy striking the back of the fire. "I think it's coming down the chimney, Henry."

The noises did indeed seem louder. There was another bang from the chimney – and then suddenly there was a tremendous rumbling and crashing and the lovely new "log effect" electric fire exploded before their eyes as some sort of large black bomb burst through it, accompanied by clouds of soot and tumbling bricks, and shot out into the middle of the room.

For some moments Cyril lay still. He was badly jolted and bruised. However, he was alive; no bones seemed broken; oxygen still hissed into the mask; the mask itself was still secure. Too secure – Cyril found he couldn't get it off. The clasp had stuck.

After a while, watched in terrified silence by Mr and Mrs Salt, Cyril struggled to his feet. He could see hardly anything at first, but as he rubbed the soot from his mask, a room began to appear. He rubbed some more, and now made out two dim figures in a bed. "Ah ha," thought Cyril, "at last."

He peered around, and soon saw his sack beside the shattered fire. He felt about in it, selected a plastic train set and a piece of cardboard with plastic dolls' furniture attached, and advanced toward the bed.

"Uf bof muh huh," said Cyril, his voice completely muffled by the oxygen mask. "Wof ha hof ca-ha-ha." Then, with a graceful bow, he placed the plastic toys on the end of the bed.

But now something even stranger happened. It seemed to Cyril that he recognized one of the people in the bed. He rubbed the face of his mask yet again and leant over to look closer.

It was Mr Salt – the Manager of Cyril's bank in Wimbledon! They had had many embarrassing talks about money together. How amazing. And that woman next to him must be his wife. Here indeed was a chance to do some good.

Cyril clanked with difficulty round the bed towards Mrs Salt. He waved his sack at her generously. "Hef hah muh huh," he said muffledly. "Hof wof ca-ha-ha." And bending close he reached to shake her hand.

However, he now saw that Mrs Salt was pressing back into the pillows. Her mouth was open as though she were trying to scream. Mr Salt, whom he remembered was in some ways a difficult man, although clearly horrified, also looked as though he might suddenly become very angry.

Cyril decided it was time to go. Yet, he couldn't just leave two ridiculous plastic presents. No – he'd leave the lot. With a bold gesture he held up the sack and emptied across the bed a noisy jumble of plastic toys and pitons, spikes, crimpons, clanks, clinks and clampons.

Then, leaving large sooty footprints on the white carpet, Cyril clanked heavily out of the room.

Unfortunately, as he was crossing the elegant drawing room, the rope which was trailing behind him became tangled round a table piled with dainty objects, bringing it crashing to the ground. Turning at the noise, Cyril blundered into another, larger table of ornaments. At the same time, one of the teeth on his boots caught the sofa cover, ripping a long tear in it.

At the door of the flat he untied the rope and managed to get out of the boots. He felt quite light again.

He was half way down the corridor when he heard a shout. Looking back, he saw dimly through the oxygen mask Mr Salt at the door of his flat. He was waving some sort of weapon. Perhaps a poker. "Hey!" shouted Mr Salt.

Cyril turned and broke into a run. He couldn't apologize for the tables now. He didn't want to talk to Mr Salt about anything at that moment. At the end of the corridor were some stairs. Panting in the mask, Cyril hurried down them.

As he arrived at the next floor, he saw the door of the lift opening. Thankfully, he dashed in.

To his astonishment, he found inside two other men dressed in Father Christmas uniform. "Get out at the wrong floor, did yer?" said one. "Stick with us, mate."

"Muh," said Cyril in a muffled voice, pulling his hood close round his head to conceal the mask.

The lift went up to the top floor. One of the men looked carefully out, but the corridor was empty. Cyril supposed that Mr Salt was still chasing him down the stairs. The two men, followed by Cyril, walked a little way down the corridor and stopped outside Flat 43. The door opened a crack, one of the men whispered something, and they were let in.

Cyril, to whom the whole night seemed more and more like some strange dream, was hardly surprised to find himself in a large room entirely filled with

Father Christmases. There must have been a hundred of them, and they all seemed to be giants. Indeed, it was his smallness – and perhaps the oxygen cylinders – which drew some curious glances towards him as he and his companions squeezed into the crowded room. Cyril drew his hood even closer together, muttered something muffled, and began to push his way towards a heavily curtained window.

Here he waited until someone at the front shouted "Attention please", when he quickly slipped behind the curtains.

He did not take long to force open the buckle and take off the mask. It was a great relief; though Cyril felt all the oxygen had somehow helped him survive his terrifying adventures. He looked out of the window. It was still dark, but growing lighter. Snow was falling on to an iron fire escape.

He turned back at the sound of clapping coming from the room. There was a chair against the window and standing on it Cyril slightly parted the curtains. He saw an odd sight.

At the far end of the room was a small stage. On to this was climbing one of the most enormous women Cyril had ever seen in his life. She had a cigarette in her large, bright red lips; and her dyed red hair frizzed out from a tiny Father Christmas hood stuck on the back of her head. In fact she bulged out everywhere from a sort of Father Christmas dress which might have been silly if she hadn't looked so terrifying to Cyril. The fat lips were cruel; the blue eyes fierce. Certainly, all the other Father Christmases were completely silent.

Cyril was later to learn that this was Madam Big – the most dangerous criminal in Europe. She looked slowly and menacingly over her quiet audience, then began to speak.

"Now listen to this," said Madam Big in a hoarse voice. So Cyril, trembling behind the curtains, learnt the plans of one of the most daring robberies of this century – the Great Father Christmas Robbery.

Gathered in that room, he discovered, were over a hundred of the boldest and most brutal criminals in England. Madam Big had got them together, and had had them made Father Christmases in all the big stores and shops all over the country. In London, Edinburgh, Manchester, Brighton, Birmingham, Liverpool, Glasgow, Southampton – in every large town and city, all the Father Christmases were now highly trained robbers. On Christmas Eve, more of these evil Father Christmases were to slip into the stores and stops. Who, as Madam Big said, would notice an extra Father Christmas or so on Christmas Eve? During that night, the gang would strike. Everything valuable in every store would be loaded on to vans and driven to waiting boats on lonely coasts or concealed in prepared hiding places. Millions upon millions of pounds' worth of goods would be stolen.

Cyril learnt much more. The password – Christmas Cracker. How much and when the gang would be paid – £25,000 each and within two months. But some questions at the end reminded him that he was now in an extremely dangerous position.

"What about the geezers that aren't in on this?"

asked a voice, which Cyril recognized as that of Pete, the Boringes Father Christmas, who had tried to kill him.

"They must be eliminated," said Madam Big. "You are all six feet tall. If there's a small Father Christmas in your store – get rid of him."

"Did yer say we was *all* big men?" came a voice from the back of the room. "All what's in the room and in the gang?"

Cyril let the curtain fall and stepped hurriedly off the chair. Several of the Father Christmases had been aware of his arrival – the oxygen cylinders had been particularly noticeable. He didn't want a search. It was time to be going.

Luckily the window opened easily and quietly. Cyril looked out nervously, but the fire escape platform was directly below him. He passed out the mask and cylinders, climbed out himself and pulled the window shut.

The wind had dropped, but it was still snowing. Cyril suddenly felt very tired indeed. He'd only slept a few hours. He staggered groggily down the fire escape. He longed to go home to bed but first he must see the police. He was also determined, once home, never to go to Boringes again.

At the bottom of the fire escape there was a dustbin. Cyril dropped the oxygen mask into it and then waved at an early morning taxi. "Scotland Yard," he said, as he climbed wearily into it.

Commissioner Henderson was the new chief at Scotland Yard. As a result, he always arrived early to work. Sometimes, as this morning, before seven o'clock. He was rather surprised to see, as his official car drew up, what looked like a man dressed as Father Christmas entering the Yard.

Commissioner Henderson started up the stairs to his office, then stopped. What *was* a Father Christmas doing in Scotland Yard? He turned round and went down the stairs.

When he arrived at the public reception some sort of row was in progress. The Father Christmas was jumping up and down and shouting. "Don't you 'Look here' me," he shouted. "I've had as much as I can stand. I haven't had a wink of sleep for several months. I've got to get home to bed. I insist on seeing the head of this place."

Commissioner Henderson walked up to the reception desk. "What's the trouble, Sergeant?" he said.

"The trouble," said the angry little Father Christmas, turning to him, "is that this fool doesn't believe me."

At the sight of the face inside the red hood, Commissioner Henderson bent down to look closely, then stepped back in astonishment.

"Cyril Bonhamy!" he cried. "Cyril Bonhamy the Writer! I've read every word you've written, sir. As a matter of fact, I write in a small way myself. At weekends. Children's books. Your last book – sensational! But why this gear, Mr Bonhamy?" Commissioner Henderson pointed to the Father Christmas uniform, streaked with soot and damp with snow. "No," said Commissioner Henderson, holding up his hand as Cyril opened his mouth. "Don't tell me. A new book – you are researching a new book. Am I right?"

"In a way," said Cyril.

"A novel, perhaps?" said the Commissioner.

"Perhaps," said Cyril.

"I'll take care of this," said the Commissioner to the Sergeant. "Mr Bonhamy is a most distinguished writer. Please come with me, Mr Bonhamy."

And so Cyril found himself telling his extraordinary story to the new Commissioner of Scotland Yard. When he'd finished, the Commissioner was looking very grave.

"Do you believe me?" said Cyril.

Commissioner Henderson nodded. He would probably have believed Cyril anyway, because he thought he was such a good writer. But in fact he'd recognized the notorious Madam Big immediately from Cyril's description. And recently there had been rumours that she was planning something very large indeed. Clearly, this was it.

"Well," said Cyril with a huge yawn. "If you'll excuse me, I simply must get home to bed."

"I don't think that would be at all a good idea," said Commissioner Henderson.

"What?" cried Cyril.

Commissioner Henderson explained that it was quite likely, from what Cyril had said, that there had been a search for him at Madam Big's flat. It was possible, since they were so close to Boringes, that Pete had guessed it might be Cyril who had been at the meeting. In which case, they could well be waiting for him at Wimbledon. For the same reason – to

59

convince Madam Big and the robbers that nothing was wrong – he wanted Cyril to go into Boringes as usual on Monday.

"But I'll be murdered," said Cyril. Commissioner Henderson explained the police had contacts with the security services at all the big stores. He'd guarantee Cyril's safety.

"Why can't you just go out and arrest them all now?" said Cyril.

"We'd lose the rest of the gang," said Commissioner Henderson, "and we need to catch them at it. Besides which, we've been after Madam Big since 1963 – you'll remember the Great Train Robbery? She's always been too clever for us. Now we have a chance."

Cyril was too tired to argue. He felt he hadn't had any proper sleep for several years. "You'd better tell Deirdre," he said, yawning again.

"I'll write a little note," said the Commissioner. "Something appropriate – of a Father Christmas nature. I told you I had some small talent in that direction."

"You'd better tell her now." Cyril yawned again, twice. "She'll be wondering why I'm not back already, after my go as night watchman."

So, as an almost asleep Cyril was led away by a kindly policeman, Commissioner Henderson drew a piece of paper towards him. For a moment he stared dreamily into space. Then, bending his head, he began to write rapidly in big, curly hand-writing, of which he was rather proud.

The Battle of Boringes

Cyril slept the whole of Sunday. He woke once, at one o'clock, for a bath and a surprisingly delicious lunch, then again, at eight o'clock, for supper. After which he slept all night. While he slept, his Father Christmas uniform was cleaned and ironed.

Commissioner Henderson, having had his note to Deirdre typed and dispatched, set up emergency plans to deal with Madam Big. A rush order was put out for three thousand Father Christmas uniforms to be ready by Tuesday morning. In every town and city, police chiefs were ordered to make immediate plans for raiding all the big stores on Christmas Eve with policemen dressed in the uniforms. Coast guards and customs men were alerted round the coast.

Commissioner Henderson had a strong feeling that Boringes was very important in Madam Big's plans. He felt sure that was why she had taken a flat so near it. A special unit of the famous S.A.S., also issued with Father Christmas uniforms, was told that it would deal with the store.

Commissioner Henderson believed that an attempt really had been made on Cyril's life. This too suggested the importance of Boringes. For this reason, when a much refreshed Cyril was dropped by a police car quite close to the store on Monday morning, a policeman dressed in the uniform of a Boringes' security guard followed a little distance behind him.

As he entered the building Cyril noticed that the cradle for cleaning the windows was now round the back again. He climbed the stairs with the security guard behind him. At the top, he pointed out the Grotto and the Wendy House. Then, with a slight sinking of heart, he stumped down the story tunnel and prepared for the day.

Cyril didn't want to be a Father Christmas any more. Nor did he find the horrid children or Mr Jessop any less irritating. But he had slept for eighteen hours, it was exciting to be helping to catch criminals, and there were reassuring glimpses of the security guard from time to time. And at lunch, mysteriously, a delicious stew was waiting for him in the Wendy House.

It was now Deirdre who began to be worried. The note that she had received on Sunday made her think that Cyril was becoming decidedly unbalanced. "Can't get back today," it had read, "having trouble getting reindeer from zoo for sledge. May spend night in sledge. Don't worry – your loving Cyril."

When he failed to return that night she decided to

ring Boringes first thing in the morning. This she did and was eventually put on to Mr Prichard. Their conversation was not entirely satisfactory.

"Is my husband Cyril Bonhamy there?" said Deirdre in an agitated voice. "Is he all right?"

"Mr Bonhamy is at his post," said Mr Prichard. "As far as I am aware he is in good health."

"Why do you make the poor man get reindeer?" said Deirdre.

"I don't know what you're talking about," said Mr Prichard.

"Well, where did he spend the night?" said Deirdre desperately.

"I'm sorry, madam," said Mr Prichard stiffly, "I cannot interfere with the private lives of employees. Where Mr Bonhamy spends his nights is entirely his own affair."

During Monday afternoon Commissioner Henderson decided that Cyril should sleep at Boringes so that he could watch out for any developments. Cyril found a note telling him this when he went into the Wendy House at the end of the day. There was also a camp bed, bedclothes, and another delicious meal with half a bottle of red wine.

Commissioner Henderson wrote several notes to Deirdre before he was satisfied. With each one he became increasingly carried away by the subject. The final one probably went further than he really meant.

"Skimming roofs in practice reindeer flight," wrote the Commissioner excitedly, "caught sledge runner in gutter. Forced to spend night down chimney – but repaired sledge in time to get to

63

work. Your loving Cyril Christmas."

Deirdre got the note in the evening and immediately rang Boringes, only to find an idiot night watchman. First thing in the morning she was on to Mr Prichard. She had an even more unsatisfactory conversation than before.

"But have you checked the roofs and chimneys?" she cried. "Have you checked the gutters?"

"No, I haven't," said Mr Prichard, "but I hardly think it likely . . ."

"But I must know where he spends the nights," wailed Deirdre.

"I'm sorry, but I told you before," said Mr Prichard coldly, "I don't know. Goodbye."

Cyril was finding Father Christmasing as difficult as ever. It was true he was now getting enough sleep, but the children seemed even more irritating than before. He swiped at several with his sack. Mothers complained. Mr Jessop appeared. Cyril, who now regarded him as no more than a common criminal, ignored him. However, he did not want to upset Mr Prichard, so from time to time he did some dandling.

One of these sessions was indeed seen by Mr Prichard, fortunately – for he had become rather curious about his Senior Father Christmas, whom he was beginning to see in a new light.

Meanwhile, back at Scotland Yard, Commissioner Henderson was settling to the task he now found the most pleasant of his day. "Crash-landed in Lapland last night," he wrote, his eyes gleaming, "while collecting sacks of toys. Luckily called in a band of my faithful gnomes and got back at dawn."

He signed this one simply "Father Christmas" and gave instructions for it to be delivered next morning.

Deirdre received it after breakfast. She read it, turned pale, then rushed to the telephone.

Mr Prichard was his usual unhelpful self, and suddenly Deirdre flew into a rage. "What are you doing to my husband?" she shrieked. "Driving him to Lapland, reindeer on the roof, chimneys. *Where does he spend the nights?*"

Mr Prichard put the telephone down firmly. "The woman's raving mad," he thought. "Poor Mr Bonhamy – no wonder he sleeps elsewhere." Then he picked up another telephone and gave some instructions to his security men.

Thus it was that later in the day Deirdre was seized, running wildly around Boringes looking for Cyril, and carried struggling from the building. Cyril himself, bored and irritated in the Grotto, heard nothing. He had begun to feel he couldn't stand the three days still to go before Christmas. In fact, terrible events had already started which were to make this unnecessary.

The first Cyril learnt of them was when he retired as usual to the Wendy House at the end of the day. Boringes shut at half-past seven on a Wednesday, and he was rather surprised not to find any delicious dinner or half bottle of red wine. Nor had lunch been cleared away. Then, while taking off his beard, he thought he heard a faint murmuring coming from behind the back wall of the Wendy House. Curious, Cyril cautiously removed the wodge of newspaper which he'd stuffed into the hole he had made with the ice pick. In the little inner room was a sight which froze his blood.

Opposite him, immediately recognizable, were the huge back and head of Madam Big. She was telephoning. Beside her stood a Father Christmas. Every now and again, at a signal from Madam Big, he stuck a flag in the map. But it was what she was saying that soon terrified Cyril even more.

"Birmingham Z2?" asked Madam Big in her hoarse voice. "This is Christmas Cracker. Operation Father Christmas to be activated immediately. Your Zone B, map reference Zh3/Hh8, is alerted. Code word changed from Christmas Cracker to Odd Beard. Out."

She put down the telephone and signalled to the man beside her to place another flag on the map. Then she dialled a new number and began speak, "Birmingham Y4? This is Christmas Cracker . . ."

Madam Big had begun to suspect something might be wrong when she learnt on Tuesday that some policemen in Ipswich had been seen parading in Father Christmas uniforms. It could have been for a party. On the other hand . . . Then there was the extra security guard who had twice turned Pete away from the Fourth Floor, when he'd come looking for Cyril. And the fact that Cyril himself, the one Father Christmas not a member of her gang, mysteriously disappeared each night.

She could have abandoned the whole plan and months of work. Instead – with typical Madam Big daring – she decided to go ahead with it immediately. She would have only one night – but a lot could be shifted in a night.

Cyril hurriedly but quietly pushed the wodge of newspaper back in the hole. He must warn Commissioner Henderson immediately. He put on his beard and tiptoed to the door of the Wendy House.

Fresh horrors were outside. The Fourth Floor was swarming with huge Father Christmases, all with armfuls of goods. Cyril pulled back his head. He'd be recognized and seized instantly.

For five minutes he sat in despair, listening to the tramp tramp of heavy feet, muffled shouts and calls. But gradually these grew fainter, and soon Cyril could hear nothing. Cautiously he peeped out of the Wendy House. The robber Father Christmases had moved farther off, towards Men's Shoes. Cyril could hear them shouting to each other. There were none in sight.

Taking a deep breath he gathered the skirts of his uniform and scuttled across from Wendy City down the present tunnel into Father Christmas Grotto.

So far so good. Now what? The Grotto was made of blue plastic. Cyril squeezed himself behind the sledge, lifted the bottom of the plastic and wriggled under it.

He found that the Grotto had been built along the back of the store, right against one of the long windows. Cyril stood up in the small space between the plastic sheet and the window and peered out.

In front of him, hanging in the night, he could see the cradle for cleaning the windows. It looked as though the part of the window in front of him could be opened. He twisted and pulled and finally a large

67

flap of the window swung upwards.

With sinking heart Cyril realized what he would have to do. There hung the cleaning cradle before him. Behind, he could just hear the shouts, much muffled, of the robber Father Christmases. To a brave, active man escape would have been quite simple. He had to do little more than step out of the window and down into the cradle.

But Cyril was not very active and he didn't feel at all brave. He gave the cradle a push and it swung away. He looked down, then pulled his head sharply back. Far far below, he'd seen the snow-covered street.

For five minutes Cyril leant out and pulled back, shut his eyes and held his breath then opened them and breathed out – trying to pluck up courage to step down out of the window.

Finally, he counted up to fifty with his eyes shut, then held his breath and somehow fell out towards the cradle.

It was absolutely terrifying. He landed heavily, flopped across the rail that went round the cradle, his head inside, his legs out. The cradle swung wildly away from the store and then swung back, so that Cyril's legs crashed through the window. It also tilted under his weight. Cyril felt himself slipping and clutched desperately at the floor of the cradle, trying to pull himself in.

Luckily, the robber Father Christmases could neither hear nor see the commotion. But several passers-by were nearly hit by falling glass. Looking up they watched in amazement as the cradle swung to and fro, a pair of small red legs wildly kicking over its side. Suddenly, with an extra lurch of the cradle, the legs disappeared inside.

For some minutes Cyril lay on the bottom of the cradle, panting. He was thinking – if I ever get back to Wimbledon alive, I shall never, ever leave it again. I shall never leave my study again. I may never leave my *bed* again.

He raised himself slowly on one knee. In the middle of the rail was the little lever he remembered the man pushing. Cyril pushed it. To his relief, the cradle silently and smoothly began to descend.

Half an hour later, Cyril was at Scotland Yard explaining as quickly as he could what had happened. Commissioner Henderson, who had been working late, listened intently. "And you say the new password is Odd Beard?"

"I think so," said Cyril.

"Right," said Commissioner Henderson. "We have no time to lose. Come with me. This may interest you."

So began the last act of the Great Father Christmas Robbery. Commissioner Henderson took Cyril to the main operations room in Scotland Yard. This was full of maps, radar screens, telephones and a mass of bewildering but exciting computer-like machinery, all of which sprang to life soon after Cyril and Commissioner Henderson arrived.

Within two hours, an army of police Father Christmases was fanning out across every big town and city in Britain. Each had a blue armband for identification, each was armed. Silently, they sur-

rounded every main department store in groups of ten or twenty, then one by one they slipped inside.

But on strict instructions from Commissioner Henderson, no store was entered until Boringes itself was under attack. He was terrified that a warning might be sent to Madam Big and she would escape.

First, five hundred ordinary policemen surrounded the big London store, keeping well out of sight. Then at twelve o'clock Commissioner Henderson gave the word and fifty crack S.A.S. troops in Father Christmas uniforms stormed in. Some descended from the roof by ropes and crashed in through windows; others let off stun bombs on the ground floor and dashed in through the smoke; still others came up through the sewers. The Battle of Boringes had begun.

The Battle of Boringes began first; it did not end first. As the night went on messages started to come in from all over Britain as store after store was recaptured: Rackhams in Birmingham (fifteen robber Father Christmases caught), Jenners in Edinburgh (twelve caught, two escaped), L. Wilkins in Calne (six caught), Debenhams in Ipswich (seven caught). But at Boringes, battle raged. Stun bombs went off repeatedly; a fire started on the First Floor; three robber Father Christmases tried to escape but were caught by the policemen surrounding the store.

Meanwhile, in Southampton Tyrell and Green was recaptured, in Manchester Kendal Milne, in Glasgow Frasers and in Bath Owen Owen.

Finally, at two o'clock, the news came that the Battle of Boringes was over: fifty robbers caught,

71

five badly injured. But as Commissioner Henderson listened to the news over the operations room radio, his face fell.

"You're sure?" he said. "Right – thank you." Then turning to the other police officers near him he said, "She's done it again. They can't find her. Madam Big has escaped."

There was a low groan from one of the police officers. The rest sat in depressed silence. Suddenly Cyril had an idea. "Have they looked in Wendy City?" he asked.

"Wendy City?" said Commissioner Henderson in a surprised voice. Cyril explained about the room with the radio equipment hidden in the middle of the Wendy Houses. At once the Commissioner got on to Boringes again.

Ten minutes later a triumphant call came from the S.A.S. – they'd got Madam Big! It had been a tremendous fight and taken eight of them – two were knocked unconscious. But the most wanted criminal in Europe was finally captured.

"Time we went down there," said Commissioner Henderson. "Come with us, Mr Bonhamy – this triumph is entirely due to you."

Although it was still dark and snowing hard, the scene round Boringes was bright as day. Powerful lights were trained on the store and its own lights blazed out from broken windows. At the far end two fire engines were fighting the fire on the First Floor. The street was full of policemen and people who had rushed out from the nearby houses and flats. Television men and reporters jostled round the main entrance. As they drew up, Cyril saw three very battered Father Christmases, their hands tied behind their backs, being hurried through the crowd and shoved roughly into a waiting police van.

Commissioner Henderson forced his way to the door, with Cyril close behind. The cameras zoomed in close and a reporter pushed a mike towards them. "Later, later," said Commissioner Henderson. "It's not over yet, you know."

Once inside, they were directed to the Fifth Floor. A stun bomb had put the lifts out of action so they had to walk.

Some of the fiercest fighting had been on the Fifth Floor. Displays lay scattered, windows were broken and there was a strong smell of smoke. It was dim because many lights had been smashed, but over to one side was a small group of men. Commissioner Henderson, strode towards them, Cyril trotting behind.

There were several members of the S.A.S., some smoking and resting on their rifles. They were all big men, but in their midst, the figure that stood out, the person Cyril noticed at once, was Madam Big. She stood with bent head, an S.A.S. man holding each arm; even when beaten, there was something frightening about her. Just behind was Mr Jessop, his hands tied behind him. In front, talking to an S.A.S. officer and looking rather wild, was Mr Prichard.

Mr Prichard had had a difficult night. He had been seized when the store closed, bound hand and foot, gagged and thrown into a cupboard. The S.A.S. had found him lying among two thousand spare Cindy Dolls, with the security guard who was supposed to

73

have given Cyril his supper. Mr Prichard had emerged to find his store half wrecked and he was in an extremely jumpy condition. As Commissioner Henderson came up, he noticed Cyril.

"Mr Bonhamy!" he cried. "Mr Bonhamy! What are you doing here?"

"It is to Mr Bonhamy that we owe the success of this entire operation," said Commissioner Henderson. He, too, was very excited. To capture Europe's most wanted criminal was a marvellous start to his career at Scotland Yard. At the same time, he didn't want to seem too pleased or to boast. Perhaps he should say a bit more about Cyril.

Commissioner Henderson got rather carried away. Cyril felt quite embarrassed. Finally, the Commissioner finished and turned to Madam Big. "And so, Madam," he said with a slight bow, "we meet at last."

But Madam Big did not answer. While Commissioner Henderson had been describing Cyril's part, she had slowly raised her head, then turned it until she had found the man who had wrecked her plans. Now she stood staring fixedly at him with her fierce blue eyes. Her face had gone a fiery red.

Commissioner Henderson, seeing the direction of her eyes, said, "And, I might add, it is entirely owing to brave Mr Bonhamy that we caught you tonight." Briefly, he described how Cyril had directed them to Wendy City.

What followed was so quick that no one there quite realized what happened. Cyril saw the two S.A.S. men holding Madam Big go flying back-

wards as though they'd been kicked by a horse. There was a gigantic flurry, and other S.A.S. men and Mr Prichard crashed to the ground. Cyril was aware of the vast figure of Madam Big about to land on him. He darted behind Commissioner Henderson, only to see this protection also swept aside. Then he found he was running at top speed across the Fifth Floor. Close behind, he heard the pounding of huge feet.

Cyril usually never ran at all, but now fear gave him an extraordinary speed; fury did the same for Madam Big. Cyril skipped round obstacles, dodging; Madam Big went straight through them like a tank. Garden furniture scattered before her.

Twice she nearly caught him. Once Cyril flung himself to one side, trapped by a climbing frame; Madam Big charged right through it, unable to stop. Another time he fell and she ran over him, one great foot just missing his head.

Now – near the end of his strength – he saw a clear space with a balcony at the end. If he could just get over that, away from her, to give the S.A.S. time to help him. He put on a last burst of panic-stricken speed.

Too late, Cyril realized it was the balcony that went round the well in the middle of the store. He was trapped. Madam Big – thirty yards behind – realized it too. Gathering the last of her tremendous strength she let out a sudden shriek of furious triumph – "Aaaaaaaaah!" shrieked Madam Big – "Ha – haaaaaaaaaah!"

Then Cyril saw a gap in the balcony, a platform. It

was the start of Mr Prichard's prize feature – the switchback from the Fifth to the Fourth floor. Shutting his eyes, he dived through.

It was terrifying. It was the most terrifying thing that had happened to him during five days that had been filled with terrifying things. He did not feel that he was sliding, but that he was falling. He seemed to fall straight down, the wind rushing through his hair. Then, abruptly, he was falling straight up. The store whirled in a blur before one open eye. And at last, trembling and gasping, Cyril landed with a thump on the platform outside Wendy City. He lay paralysed, staring above him.

Had he looked back over the well, he would have seen a sight as strange and terrifying as his own extraordinary descent. Seeing Cyril disappear Madam Big tried to stop – but she was no more able to stop than a mad rhinoceros. She crashed through the balcony and fell on to the narrow slide.

By some miracle it did not break – though it swayed and sagged and one support buckled in the middle. But the great bulk of Madam Big gathered too much speed. She hurtled down, then hurtled up – going faster every split second. At the end she was going far too fast to stop. She simply took off – Cyril had the impression of something big, a mattress with outstretched arms, skimming over him. She flew out above Wendy City, over the intervening space, and crashed down on the other side.

There was a loud report and then, in a series of rippings and crackings, the Father Christmas Grotto collapsed on top of her.

Home Again

There is really very little more to tell. Later that night – or rather, early in the morning of the next day – Cyril was driven back to Wimbledon.

Deirdre had been given some strong Slogodon sleeping pills by her doctor and took a little while to wake up. But when she did, and realized it was Cyril, she burst into tears. "Oh, darling," she cried, "where have you been?"

"Don't worry," said Cyril, "I'll tell you later. Everything's all right."

In the morning, over an enormous breakfast, he told her the whole story. Deirdre was amazed – and very impressed. "There you are," she said. "I told you you were good at other things besides books."

"Well – perhaps," said Cyril modestly.

Then she showed him the notes that Commissioner Henderson had sent her and said how worried

78

she'd been. Cyril agreed the notes were rather odd, but they decided not to mention it. "I expect he got carried away," said Cyril.

For the next four days Cyril was in practically all the newspapers. He appeared on ten television programmes and eleven radio programmes. The telephone went all day with people asking questions, and telegrams of congratulations poured in. His publisher rang up and said they'd decided to bring out all his books again as he'd become so popular.

Best of all, the owners of the big stores got together and decided to give Cyril a cheque for £25,000 as a reward for preventing the robbery.

The award took place in the evening at Boringes. Commissioner Henderson was there to make a speech; also Mr Prichard, who was to give Cyril the cheque. Deirdre decided not to go. She had not quite forgiven either Commissioner Henderson, or Mr Prichard. However, she watched the whole thing on telly. They had made Cyril put on his Father Christmas uniform. "For the last time," said Cyril.

Mr Prichard made a long speech about there being No Limit to the Boringes Serivce; how Mr Bonhamy had been the best Father Christmas they had ever had, and how nothing Mr Bonhamy could do would ever surprise him. Then he handed over the cheque and everyone clapped and cheered and they opened champagne. Cyril had several large glasses.

Some time later, he arrived back at Wimbledon.

"Oh, Cyril," said Deirdre, holding up the cheque, "it's even better than that time you were kidnapped by those Arabs.★ You *are* clever."

Cyril took off his beard and pushed back the hood. "Now to get out of this," he said.

"Oh, Cyril," said Deirdre.

"Mmmm?" said Cyril, struggling to get out of the Father Christmas uniform.

"Cyril – could you just keep it on a *little* longer?" said Deirdre.

Cyril stopped struggling. "Why?" he said in a muffled voice.

"You know that nice photographer Mr Hornach down the road who has eleven children? Well, he and his wife Laura are giving a children's party tonight and I promised you'd go as Father Christmas. He's built a special false chimney for you to slide down."

Cyril, who'd given a nervous jump at the word "chimney" suddenly thought – well, why not? What was a chimney, especially a false chimney, to the man who'd broken the Great Father Christmas gang, who'd virtually single-handed captured Madam Big?

"All right," he said, pulling the hood back over his head and tucking the beard behind his ears.

And so they set off into the night together; Deirdre so tall and loving, Cyril small, swaying slightly from the champagne, his Father Christmas uniform still too large and now looking extremely battered.

★ To read about Cyril's adventures with the Arabs, see *The Terrible Kidnapping of Cyril Bonhamy* (Evans, 1978).